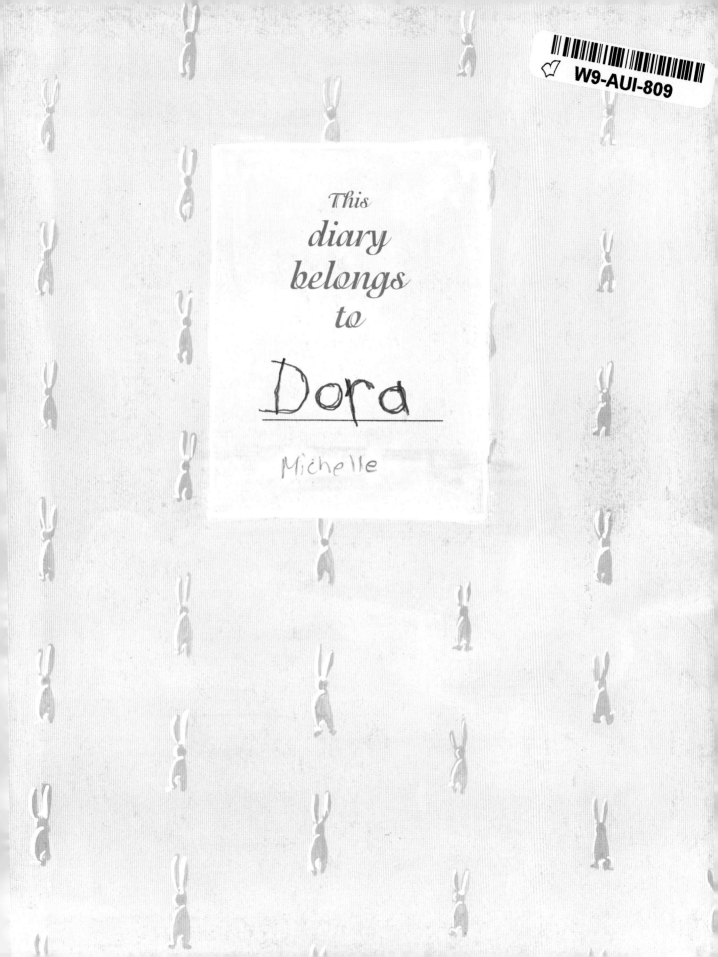

This
diary
belongs
to

Dora

Michelle

My name is Dora and I'm mostly brown.

YOU'RE #1

(I think I'm part cottontail.)

And this is my best friend, Ally, she gave me this diary.

Ally

We are inseparable

(at least that's what my Mom says)

We even sit next
to each other in
school.

Go Harding Hares

(That other girl
is BABBETTE.)

Babbette thinks she looks just like the Easter bunny.

Babbette is **not** my best friend!

She and her friends play with dolls.

I think dolls are boring

Me and Ally play pretend alot.

Like our scooters are
wild horses,
or Ally is stuck
in quicksand and
I have to save her

Or if we don't get our
puzzle finished in time
it will
explode
and pollute
the world!

And when we're not together
we e-mail each other
all the time.

Sunday—

I went to Ally's house to play but she wasn't there.

I couldn't believe it!

We always played on Sunday.

I waited for her and when she finally came home she was carrying → a doll!

I yelled, "Ugg, why do you have that?! Dolls don't do anything, they just open and close their eyes and drink and wet!"... Ally didn't say anything, she just took her doll and went inside.

Sunday wasn't a very fun day.

Monday morning—

Yuck, and I thought yesterday was
bad! No one was waiting for me
outside school except that quiet
girl, Rose.

Then during art class Babbette
passed a note to Ally.
When I jumped and grabbed it
I spilled paint all over everything.
Rose said she liked my
painting, it looked like modern
art.

But everyone else
just
laughed.

Monday-after lunch...

When I read the note my worst fears came true!

To Ally

A L L Y   A L L Y

A L L Y   A L L Y

At recess I told Ally it was me or icky Babbette. Ally said I was no fun so she went to play with Babbette. I spent the rest of recess pretending I was going down a spooky spiral staircase to a castle's gloomy dungeon.

Tuesday –
Today was even worse.

At lunch I pretended I was a prisoner chained up with bread and water and rats as my only friends while Ally and Babbette sat together and talked about baby bottles!

"What do you say

Wednesday + no change =
TERRIBLE!

Play is no fun-

1. Quicksand: I can't pretend I'm in it because there is no one to pull me out.
2. Exploding puzzle: It's hard to panic over a puzzle when I'm all alone.
3. Wild horses: No trail pardner, NO fun.
4. Dolls: I tried playing with one. Gave it a bottle. It wet... boring.

And after school I didn't have any e-mails in my mail box.

IT FEELS LIKE MONDAY EVERY DAY!

Thursday-
Morning-

Yuck, more of the same...
I pretended I was a secret
agent getting information for
a special mission.

1. number of times
Ally and Babbette
passed notes
||| = 3

2. number of times
they laughed at
each others jokes
||||| = 5

★ 3. number of times
Babbette talked
about baby dolls
|||| |||| ||| = 16 times!!

how can Ally stand it?!

Is Rose collecting information too?

UPDATE!!

At recess I was playing dungeon again. Rose came up and asked me what I was doing. I said I was going down a spiral staircase to a dungeon. Then she asked me what I'd do when I got there. I said I didn't know cause I wasn't there yet. Then she surprised me! She said she knew there was an evil wizard in the castle's tower so maybe we should go up and do battle with him.

Rose

me going down pretend dungeon stairs

continued –

WoW, it was GREAT!

After that we pretended we were cowboys trying to control a stampede. We stopped the herd right before it almost trampled Babbette and her friends.
My horse had to take a flying leap over Ally since it was galloping <u>so</u> fast.

Cowboy Dan by Jack Rudd

Friday-
Today was the greatest !!

During lunch:
1. Rose and I did the bunny hop in the lunch line.

2. Made paper hats and modeled them.

3. Pretended our milkstraws were chopsticks.

I didn't manage to eat much so now I'm a little hungry, but that's o.k.

yum yum!

小学校入学までに ひとりで、素早く

赤ちゃんおめでとうございます

お手数ですが不欄は記入の上、ご投函ください。みなさま

When I got home I got
this secret e-mail.

Dear Dora,

Three bunnies can finish an exploding puzzle
much faster than two.   Maybe tomorrow I can
come over and help you and Rose.

:)

Saturday—

Guess who came over
to help Rose and me
save the _world_ !!!